Mummy Mayhem

'Mummy Mayhem'
An original concept by Katie Dale
© Katie Dale 2024

Illustrated by Joy Dawood

Published by MAVERICK ARTS PUBLISHING LTD
Suite 1, Hillreed House, 54 Queen Street,
Horsham, West Sussex, RH13 5AD
© Maverick Arts Publishing Limited September 2024
+44 (0)1403 256941

A CIP catalogue record for this book is available at the British Library.

ISBN 978-1-83511-035-5

Printed in India

www.maverickbooks.co.uk

WEST NORTHAMPTONSHIRE COUNCIL	
60000562114	
Askews & Holts	
CC	

This book is rated as: White Band (Guided Reading)

Mummy Mayhem

By Katie Dale

Illustrated by Joy Dawood

Chapter 1

"Which way is the Cairo museum?" Omar asked excitedly, hurrying out of the hotel. He'd always wanted to visit Egypt—home of the Pharaohs, the Sphinx… and his own ancestors! "Did you know it's the largest museum in Africa?" Omar added, grinning at his dads.

"You may have mentioned it," Papa laughed.

"Once or twice," Dad added, grinning. "This way! Our guide's meeting us at the museum at midday."

The museum was amazing. Omar gazed at the golden statues, treasures and coffins.

"Can you believe these coffins are thousands of years old?" he gasped. "And there are actual mummies inside? How cool!"

Papa shuddered. "Creepy, more like!"

Omar rolled his eyes. "It's not! It's incredible! The Ancient Egyptians spent *seventy days* treating the bodies to preserve them—they believed it was the only way for people to enter the afterlife."

"Wow!" Dad smiled, impressed.

Suddenly, Omar heard a strange voice.

"Help!"

He looked around, but he and his dads were the only people in the room.

"Did you hear that?" Omar said.

Dad frowned. "I didn't hear anything."

"Help me!" cried the voice.

"There it is again!" Omar cried. "It sounded like... it was coming from this coffin..."

Papa turned pale. "Very funny!"

"Good one!" Dad chuckled. "They've got crocodile coffins in the next room! Imagine mummifying a crocodile!"

"Eek!" Papa winced and Dad laughed as they moved on.

Omar was about to follow when he heard the voice again.

"Help!"

Goosebumps prickled down Omar's arms as he leaned closer to the coffin…

"HELP!" the voice shouted suddenly.

Startled, Omar tripped over the rope barrier and fell against the coffin, which immediately sprang open!

Chapter 2

Omar froze. He was staring at a mummy! A real Ancient Egyptian mummy!

"Finally!" the mummy cried. "I've been stuck in there for four thousand years waiting for one of my descendants to let me out!"

"Descendants?" Omar frowned.

The mummy nodded. "Only my bloodline can open our coffins, so you and I must be related!"

"Really?!" Omar said excitedly. "My family *is* originally from Egypt!"

"Nice to meet you," The mummy beamed. "I'm Seti."

Omar smiled uncertainly. "Hi Seti… Umm, are you… not alive?"

"That's right!" the mummy laughed. "I'm dead. Very. But I had a good life."

"I'm glad," Omar smiled. "I'm Omar."

"Hi Omar. I need your help," Seti begged. "If I don't get back to my pyramid, I'll never be reunited with my family in the afterlife!"

"Oh no!" Omar cried. "Of course I'll help you!"

"Let's go!" Seti cried, striding across the room.

"Wait!" Omar cried. "You need a disguise!"

Omar hurried to the museum's lost and found room.

"My dad left some clothes here yesterday," he fibbed, rifling through the box anxiously until he found what he needed. "Bingo!"

Omar dashed back to Seti.

"Better?" Seti asked, trying the robes on.

Omar frowned. Seti's face was still exposed!

"Hang on!" Omar grabbed a scarf and sunglasses from his bag... Just in time!

"Omar, there you are!" Dad cried, returning with Papa. "What's keeping you?"

13

"I…" Omar hesitated, "…bumped into… our tour guide, Seti! He arrived early!"

"How wonderful!" Dad cried, reaching to shake Seti's hand.

"He hates being touched!" Omar cried, hastily jumping in the way. Dad had a very firm handshake and, after thousands of years in a coffin, Seti's hand might just shake right off!

"To the pyramids!" Seti cried, hurrying out of the museum—straight into the busy road!

"Stop!" Omar yelled, yanking him back onto the pavement just as a car whizzed past!

"What was that beast?" Seti gasped, trembling in shock.

"That beast," Dad sighed wistfully, "is the car of my dreams."

"You've got to be careful!" Omar hissed to Seti. "If your body gets destroyed, you'll never be reunited with your family!"

Seti nodded anxiously. "We have to get to the pyramids, quick!"

"What's the rush?" Dad chuckled. "They're not going anywhere! Besides, I've booked us on a boat ride first! Come on!"

Chapter 3

The boat ride was amazing. The white sails billowed, the River Nile sparkled and they even spotted a crocodile, much to Papa's fright!

"What's that building, Seti?" Dad asked, pointing to a shiny skyscraper.

Seti panicked and Omar gulped. Seti wouldn't know the answer; there weren't any skyscrapers when Seti was alive four thousand years ago!

"Oh, you told me that one already, didn't you, Seti?" Omar fibbed quickly. "It's the um… Grand… Nile… Tower!"

"Nice." Dad nodded.

"Can you tell us more about the Nile?" Papa asked, sipping from his cup of water.

"Of course," Seti smiled. "The god of the Nile is Sobek. He has the head of a crocodile and represents fertility, medicine... and sudden death."

Papa turned pale. "I wish I hadn't asked," he muttered. He jumped up as the boat approached the riverbank. "Dry land at last!"

But as the boat jolted against the dock, Papa's water spilled all over Seti!

"Oh no!" Seti yelped, horrified.

"Quick!" Omar said, spotting a nearby restaurant. "Let's go inside and clean you up!"

"Great idea!" Dad cried. "I'm starving!"

Omar and Seti dashed to the empty restaurant loos.

"Oh no!" Seti wailed. "If I get wet, my body will disintegrate!"

"Give me the wet robes!" Omar cried. "This'll dry you!" He jabbed the hand-drier on.

The hot air blasted Seti, blowing his bandages loose!

Double oh no!

"Omar?" Papa's voice called, as he pushed the door open. "Are you okay?"

Triple oh no!

Chapter 4

Omar hastily shoved Seti into a cubicle and shut the door, just as Papa entered the room!

"We're fine!" Omar said. "I'm just drying Seti's robes!"

Papa grimaced. "I'm so sorry, Seti! Here, I'll do that." He grabbed the robes from Omar.

"I'll do it!" Omar insisted.

"No, you go back to Dad, Omar." Papa said firmly.

Omar panicked. He couldn't let Papa see Seti without his disguise! Seti's secret would be out, and Papa was such a scaredy-cat he might have a heart attack!

"Well just… throw the robes over the cubicle door when they're dry," Omar said. "Seti doesn't let anyone see him without his robes."

Omar joined Dad at a table and waited anxiously.

"It's all traditional Egyptian food!" Dad cried, reading the menu. "I don't know what to order!"

Finally, Seti and Papa returned, and Omar breathed a sigh of relief.

"Why are there weapons on the table?" Seti whispered to Omar, looking at the cutlery nervously.

Omar giggled. "No, they're—" he began.

"I'd kill for a decent steak," Dad exclaimed.

Seti grabbed his knife and fork, holding them defensively. "I'll protect you, Omar!"

Papa and Dad stared at him.

"Ha ha!" Omar forced a laugh. "What a joker! No need to hurt anyone today—unless Dad pinches my food!" he jabbed his fork at Dad's hand playfully.

"I won't, I promise!" Dad laughed. "What would everyone like to eat? Seti?"

"Oh, I've... already eaten," Seti replied quickly. "Plus, I don't have a stomach anymore!" he whispered to Omar, and winked. "But I can recommend the Molokhiya—a traditional Egyptian stew—and honey-sweetened cakes. They're delicious!"

Dad beamed. "Thanks, Seti!"

Chapter 5

After Dad had eaten three helpings of Molokhiya and lots of honey cakes, they finally hailed a taxi.

"Pyramids, here we come!" Omar cried.

"Do you want to visit the Great Sphinx first?" the driver asked. "It's on the way!"

"Ooh yes please!" Papa cried.

Omar sighed, and shrugged apologetically at Seti, who stared out of the window. As the pyramids appeared in the distance he sighed, wistfully. Omar felt so sorry for him. He couldn't imagine being separated from his dads for a week, let alone four thousand years.

As they approached the Sphinx, Seti gasped in horror. "It didn't used to look like that!"

"Really?" Papa said. "What did it look like before?"

"It had a nose!" Seti said. "And a long braided beard, and it was painted in bright colours! The face and body were red, the beard was blue and the headdress was yellow."

Dad smiled. "Sounds amazing!"

"It was," Seti sighed. "It really was."

Finally, they reached the pyramids.

"There it is!" Seti cried excitedly. "That's my pyramid!"

"*Your* pyramid?" Dad chuckled.

"My… favourite pyramid, I mean!" Seti corrected hastily. "It took ten thousand men thirty years to build."

"Ten thousand *slaves*," Papa muttered.

"They weren't slaves!" Seti exclaimed indignantly. "The pyramids were built by well-fed, skilled labourers."

Papa blushed.

"It was originally covered with white limestone," Seti said wistfully. "It gleamed in the sunlight, like a beautiful pearl."

"Wow," Dad said. "I'm so glad you're our guide, Seti. It's like you were actually there!"

Omar and Seti grinned at each other.

Seti beamed. "I'm very glad I met you all too. But it's time for me to go home."

Omar nodded and smiled. "Goodbye, Seti."

Everyone waved as Seti disappeared behind the pyramid.

"Oh no!" Papa gasped, grabbing his wallet. "I forgot to give Seti a tip!" He hurried after him.

"No—wait!" Omar cried, chasing Papa...

…But there was no sign of Seti anywhere.

Papa gazed around the empty desert, confused. Omar spotted the robes, scarf and sunglasses behind a rock, and stuffed them into his bag.

"Where did Seti go?" Dad asked, frowning.

"To be with his family," Omar said, beaming as he took his dads' hands. "After all, what better place to be?"

The End

Book Bands for Guided Reading

The Institute of Education book banding system is a scale of colours that reflects the various levels of reading difficulty. The bands are assigned by taking into account the content, the language style, the layout and phonics. Word, phrase and sentence level work is also taken into consideration.

Maverick Early Readers are a bright, attractive range of books covering the pink to white bands. All of these books have been book banded for guided reading to the industry standard and edited by a leading educational consultant.

To view the whole Maverick Readers scheme, visit our website at www.maverickearlyreaders.com

Or scan the QR code above to view our scheme instantly!